I0605339

World of Art

Exploring COMIC ART

John Allen

San Diego, CA

Printed in the United States

For more information, contact:
ReferencePoint Press, Inc.
PO Box 27779
San Diego, CA 92198
www.ReferencePointPress.com

LIBRARY OF CONGRESS CATALOGING-IN-PUBLICATION DATA

Names: Allen, John, 1957- author.
Title: Exploring comic art / by John Allen.
Description: San Diego, CA : ReferencePoint Press, Inc., 2025. | Series: World of art | Includes bibliographical references and index.
Identifiers: LCCN 2023056849 (print) | LCCN 2023056850 (ebook) | ISBN 9781678208585 (library binding) | ISBN 9781678208592 (ebook)
Subjects: LCSH: Comic books, strips, etc.--Juvenile literature.
Classification: LCC NC1764 .A45 2025 (print) | LCC NC1764 (ebook) | DDC 741.5--dc23/eng/20231218
LC record available at https://lccn.loc.gov/2023056849
LC ebook record available at https://lccn.loc.gov/2023056850

Contents

Telling Stories with Pictures and Words

For the heroine of his team's science-fiction comic book series *The Bestiary Chronicles*, writer Steve Coulson knew what he wanted. However, with his lack of drawing skill, Coulson needed help. He described the look he wanted to the artificial intelligence (AI) art-generation tool Midjourney as a "Hitchcock blonde." By this he meant the sort of cool blonde actress who starred in Alfred Hitchcock's suspense films. The heroine that Midjourney produced looked a lot like Grace Kelly, an actress who appeared in several Hitchcock productions. In fact, the AI program used the team's detailed prompts (short text instructions) to create the whole story. The images it produced, ranging from the Massachusetts witchcraft trials of the late 1600s to the modern era and the creation of the atom bomb, combined solid storytelling with stylistic verve. It created dramatic art, including a number of futuristic monsters. Midjourney even filled in the dialogue balloons. Coulson and his team were impressed. "By the new year, even the trained eye probably won't be able to perceive an AI generation from any other," says Coulson. "It's exciting and terrifying at the same time. But you can't put the genie back in the bottle, so we're embracing the future as fast as we can."[1]

Telling Stories in Pictures and Words

Coulson's *Bestiary Chronicles* is the latest advancement in comic art. Comics are a medium that tells stories in sequence using both pictures and words. The art form dates back to political cartoons and newspaper comic strips of the 1890s. Since then it has undergone many changes. For example, genres come and go depending on what appeals to current readers. Adventure tales, crime stories, romance, war, horror, funny animals, and even classic literature have filled the pages of monthly comics. Once considered merely an amusement for children, comic books today are accepted as real artistic creations. Some comics, called graphic novels, have even earned prestigious literary awards. For example, Art Spiegelman's *Maus*, a cat-and-mouse allegory of the Holocaust, won a Pulitzer Prize in 1992.

WORDS IN CONTEXT

prompt: A short text instruction for an AI program

In recent years comics have also been adapted into movie franchises based on their characters. Comic books starring superheroes such as Batman and Captain America, which once sold for twelve cents, have inspired blockbuster films that have raked in billions at the box office worldwide. In fact, in today's entertainment world where nothing seems to last, comic book characters have shown remarkable staying power. Many of today's most popular characters, including Superman and Wonder Woman, have appeared in their own comics continuously for more than eighty years.

Comic Book Artists at Work

The status of comic book artists has also changed over the decades. Most early artists worked anonymously for publishers who paid them a rock-bottom per-page fee. Unlike the creators of newspaper strips, comic book artists generally did not own the rights to the characters they invented. Even the best artists, such as Jack "King" Kirby, toiled for long hours to meet deadlines and changed companies frequently. Only in the 1980s and 1990s did the top artists and writers start to demand, and win, higher compensation in the form of royalties, or a percentage of sales. Today a midlevel comic book artist makes from $31,000 to $50,000 a year. However, artists who develop a distinctive style and attract a fan base—which almost guarantees higher sales—can command fees approaching six figures.

> **WORDS IN CONTEXT**
>
> **storyboard: A rough layout of comic pages**

Although comic artists can use computer software and AI programs in their work, many still rely on pencil, paper, ink pen, paintbrush, and other traditional tools. A comic artist must combine a talent for drawing with a feel for dramatic presentation, like a movie director. Each image is chosen to create an emotional effect. The artist begins by making a rough storyboard with sketches for each page. This shows how the panels will be laid out and how the images will unfold. Using the storyboard, the artist makes the final drawings in pencil. The finished pages are then ready to be inked, colored, and lettered by the artist or by other hands.

Artists for the major comics companies average about one page a day and twenty pages in a month, although with practice some can draft their pages even faster. Working twelve hours a day and six days per week is not uncommon in order to meet tight deadlines in the comics industry. "You usually have 20-ish pages to submit in a month, and whatever is in the script needs to be visualized on paper," says Casey Coller, a veteran comic artist. "You also are essentially the director, actor, makeup, lighting, set designer, etc. all bundled into one pencil-wielding package. . . . It's much more involved than just drawing pretty pictures."[2]

An Industry Full of Opportunities

The comics industry offers plenty of opportunities for aspiring artists. In 2022 the global market for comic books was valued at

Blockbuster films like Captain America: The Winter Soldier *(shown) feature characters that first appeared in comic books that were published decades before the film.*

$15.5 billion. This uniquely American art form continues to change and develop. Once sold at newsstands and on drugstore spinner racks, comic books are now marketed at shops offering special events and collectors' editions with variant covers. Online comics enable fans to enjoy their favorite titles on a tablet or smartphone. Comics blogs and YouTube channels feature in-depth reviews of each month's titles. Amid all the change, comic book artists remain the linchpin of the art form. "Writers and artists make comics what they are," says comics critic Cole Kennedy, "and most of the success or praise should be attributed to their hard work."[3]

A History of Comics from Newsstands to Specialty Shops

For fifteen years Mark Michaelson kept a secret hidden away in a cardboard box. It was a secret that would especially interest his wife, Sara, who shared Mark's passion for comic books. Inside the box was an old comic he had bought from a Houston oil executive forty years before. When he finally showed it to Sara, she was astounded. It was *Superman* #1, published in 1939. The cover showed the flying superhero in all his blue-and-red, primary-colors glory. Mark offered to let Sara hold the precious item, but she did not dare risk it. "I'm not touching that," she said, only half joking. "Put it back."[4]

Her concern was understandable. In a December 2021 auction, the sixty-four-page comic sold for $2.6 million, which was quite a jump from its original cover price of ten cents. It was not the rarest of old comics—about 165 copies still exist—but it was the first comic book named for a superhero, and Michaelson's copy was kept in very good condition. The comic's sale represented a huge windfall for Michaelson, who collects comics and brokers comic book sales as a side hustle. Some of the stacks of old comics that he evaluates for clients are worth more than a new car. But Michaelson and other fans like him love comics for their history and their place in American culture. That oil executive had asked him to take care of his *Superman* comic, and Michaelson was proud to have done so for four decades. "I was very lucky to have it," he says. "But now, my 40 years is up. I just hope somebody else enjoys it."[5]

Comic Strips in the Newspaper Wars

The history of American comics goes back to the nineteenth century. Editorial cartoons in newspapers often featured dialogue balloons with cutting remarks on the day's political issues. However, it was the artwork that made the cartoons so popular. The European immigrants pouring into cities on the East Coast might have struggled to read English, but they could enjoy the witty drawings. In the newspaper wars of the 1890s, with upstart papers vying for attention, comic strips became a real selling point. One of the first comic strips to become widely popular was *Hogan's Alley*, which appeared in the *New York World* beginning in 1895. Its main character was a bald-headed Irish street kid named Mickey Dugan. His slang-filled comments were printed on his long yellow nightshirt. Readers soon began referring to the strip simply as *The Yellow Kid*.

Other newspapers added their own Sunday supplement sections with comic strips. In 1897 Rudolph Dirks created *The Katzenjammer Kids*, about two mischievous German Americans, for William Randolph Hearst's *New York Journal*. The strip not only made kids' high jinks the focal point, it also introduced comics shorthand such as horizontal lines and dust clouds to show speed and sweat drops for fear or anxiety. Another Hearst favorite was George Herriman's *Krazy Kat*, which first appeared in 1913. It worked a thousand variations on a simple idea: Ignatz Mouse would throw a brick at Krazy Kat's head—even though Krazy was in love with Ignatz—and then get hauled off to jail by Officer Pupp. Herriman's style and humor influenced cartoonists from Walt Disney to Bill Watterson, creator of *Calvin and Hobbes*.

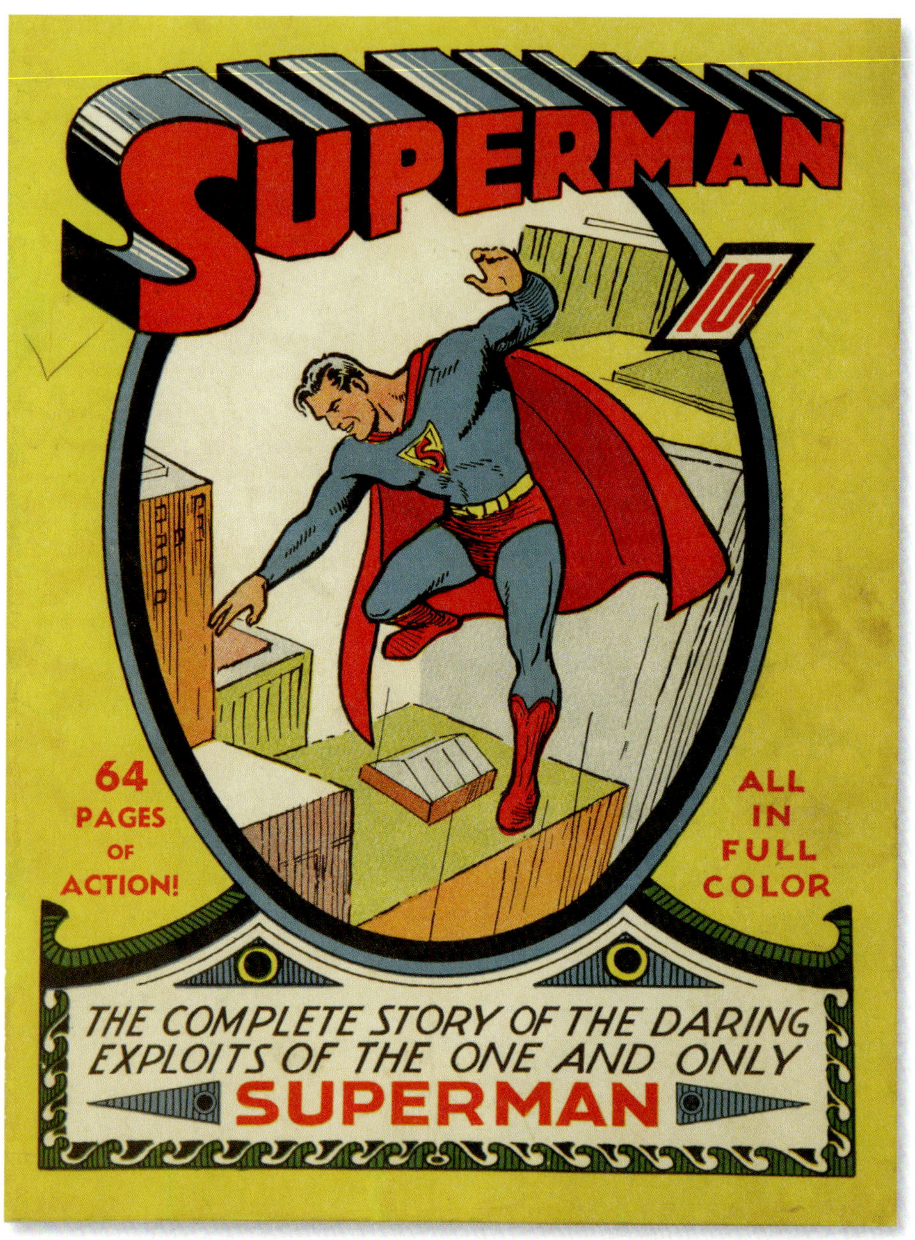

The first comic book featuring Superman, in his now iconic blue and red costume, was published in 1939.

The Advent of Comic Books and Superheroes

By the 1920s and 1930s, the most popular newspaper comic strips were attracting millions of readers. Artists signed deals with newspaper syndicates to have their strips appear in papers across

WORDS IN CONTEXT

syndicate: A group of businesses that combine for a common purpose

the nation. People were reading the same comic strips and learning the same catchphrases. "Americans began to talk about 'keeping up with the Joneses,' using the title of a successful syndicated comic strip about a family obsessed with appearing as prosperous and happy as the neighbors,"[6] says Julia Guarneri, a historian at the University of Cambridge. Strips covered a wide range of genres and subject matter, including suburban family (*Blondie*), backwoods comedy (*Li'l Abner*), crime stories (*Dick Tracy*), and science fiction (*Flash Gordon* and *Buck Rogers*). Most artists developed their own plain, recognizable style, but some strips, such as Hal Foster's *Prince Valiant*, featured beautifully detailed art with a cinematic sweep.

Struggling through the Depression, publishers began to cash in on the comic strip phenomenon by reprinting them in magazines for newsstand sales. In the late 1930s publishers began hiring artists to create comic books with original stories. Many

Making Off with the Rights to Batman

Early comic book artists toiled in obscurity for small per-page fees. Generally, they did not even own the rights to the characters they created. Under the terms of their work agreement, everything they produced belonged to the publisher. Jerry Siegel and Joe Shuster famously lost all rights to Superman by signing a release form when they first sold their stories to the publisher that became DC Comics.

However, some comic artists managed to obtain better deals. One of these was Bob Kane, the artist who created Batman along with writer Bill Finger. It was actually Finger who came up with the character's iconic cowl, cape, bat gadgets, dark color scheme, and secret identity. But Kane negotiated his own rights to get a percentage of all of DC's licensing revenue for Batman, an agreement that paid off handsomely. "Finger made Batman what he is, and had a hand in the creation of Robin, and villains like the Joker, Penguin, and Two-Face," says comic historian Daniel Rennie. "Nonetheless, Kane got all the credit. For the rest of Finger's life, and for 15 years after his death, Kane did everything he could to suppress Finger's involvement. . . . Finger, on the other hand, died penniless and in obscurity."

Daniel Rennie, "Did Bob Kane Steal Batman from Bill Finger?," Bold Entrance, March 24, 2020. https://boldentrance.com.

had characters inspired by radio shows and pulp magazines, such as the spooky crime fighter known as the Shadow. In 1938 writer Jerry Siegel teamed up with artist Joe Shuster to present a new type of hero—in fact, a superhero: Superman. He first appeared in *Action Comics* #1. The famous cover, which enthralled kids everywhere, showed Superman lifting a car over his head while crooks ran away in a panic. The character was a huge hit from the start, with *Action Comics* and *Superman* comics flying off the newsstands. Unfortunately, Siegel and Shuster had already sold the rights to the character for $130. It was not the last time that comics creators would be shortchanged for their work.

The success of Superman led to a parade of superheroes and costumed crime fighters. In 1939 Batman debuted in the pages of *Detective Comics* (later shortened to *DC Comics*). Soon the caped crusader was tangling with his own rogues' gallery of villains—the Joker, the Penguin, and Two-Face—that were inspired by Dick Tracy's weird and colorful adversaries. More superheroes followed in the next decade, such as the Flash, Green Lantern, Hawkman, the Spectre, and Black Canary. DC Comics even introduced the first superhero team, called the Justice Society of America. Superman and Batman would remain DC's chief moneymakers for decades to come.

Alongside the superheroes were comic books to suit every taste. They included adventure stories, westerns, war comics, ghost stories, and science fiction. *Walt Disney's Comics* starred cartoon favorites such as Mickey Mouse and Donald Duck. *Pep Comics* introduced a teenager named Archie Andrews and his friends Betty, Veronica, and Jughead. There were even versions of literary classics in comic book form.

As Adolf Hitler's armies rampaged across Europe, comic artists responded with patriotic superheroes. In 1941 the first issue of Timely Comics' *Captain America* hit newsstands. Its iconic cover showed the shield-carrying Captain America socking Hitler in the jaw. The Jewish heritage of writer Joe Simon and artist Jack Kirby gave the team special incentive to enlist their new character in the fight against Nazism. Also in 1941, DC Comics introduced Wonder Woman, an Amazon princess sent to help America fight the Nazis. Creator Charles Moulton (pen name for William Moulton Marston) brought a feminist viewpoint to Wonder Woman's adventures. He saw that each issue of *Wonder Woman* comics included a feature about famous women in history. "Wonder Woman isn't only an Amazonian with badass boots," says Jill Lepore, author of

In 1941, DC Comics introduced Wonder Woman, whose mission was to help America fight Germany's Nazis. The character's creator, Charles Moulton, made sure that each issue of Wonder Woman *included a feature about famous women in history.*

The Secret History of Wonder Woman. "She's the missing link in a chain of events that begins with the women's suffrage campaigns of the 1910s and ends with the troubled place of feminism fully a century later. Feminism made Wonder Woman."[7]

A Lurch Toward Crime and Horror

After World War II, sales of superhero comics sagged badly. Perhaps with all the stories of real heroes at home and abroad, the costumed variety held less appeal. Plus, a generation of comic book readers had grown up. Now other genres took over the marketplace. In 1947 Simon and Kirby broke new ground with *Young Romance* #1, a romance comic aimed at adolescent girls. The new title took off at once, selling 97 percent of its print run and sparking a flood of imitations.

> **WORDS IN CONTEXT**
>
> **genre: A category of literary creation**

Another hot genre was crime comics. Stories ranged from true-crime accounts supposedly based on police files to tales of small-time gangsters and hoods. A character like Spy Smasher, who had been fighting Nazis, now pursued American criminals as Crime Smasher. The lurid nature of these stories, however, could not match the blood and mayhem of the new horror comics. A group called Educational Comics, or EC Comics, cornered the market on horror beginning in the late 1940s. EC publisher William Gaines and his staff of hardworking artists produced comics such as *The Vault of Horror*, *Tales from the Crypt*, and *The Haunt of Fear*. Tales were introduced by wisecracking, pun-filled characters like the Crypt-Keeper and the Old Witch. Some of the stories had supernatural elements, but more often they focused on grisly revenge and murder. In the pages of EC horror comics, severed heads, rotting corpses, and scattered body parts ruled the day—or night.

Inevitably, there was a backlash. In the early 1950s, psychologists, social critics, schoolteachers, and parents claimed that comics were warping the minds of America's children. A rise in juvenile delinquency nationwide was blamed in part on comic books like *Thrilling Crime Cases* and *The Vault of Horror*. In April 1954 the US Senate held hearings that brought the accusations about comics to public attention. The hearings led publishers to adopt the Comics Code Authority (CCA) of the Comics Magazine Association of America. An independent review board had to pass each comic before it could be published with the CCA seal. Gaines chose to abandon his comic book line rather than abide by the code. He kept publishing only one item, a humor title named *Mad*, which later became *Mad* magazine.

Return of the Superheroes

The remainder of the 1950s saw a focus on science fiction and tales of gigantic monsters in response to the nuclear age. By 1961 Stan Lee, toiling away at Atlas Comics, felt he had hit a dead end in story ideas. When he threatened to quit the comics business, his wife urged him to try one last time to write the kind of comics story that

The Rise of Manga

One of today's best-selling forms of comics in America is imported from Japan. Manga, which means "whimsical stories" in Japanese, are comics originally derived from nineteenth-century Japanese woodcuts. Unlike American comic books, genuine manga is read from right to left, like the Japanese language. Manga published outside Japan generally has the pages and panels flipped to accommodate non-Japanese readers.

The modern explosion of manga in Japan began in the late 1940s, just as Japanese society was undergoing large postwar changes. The influence of American comics led the founding manga artist Osamu Tezuka to create his own distinctive heroes, like Astro Boy and Kimba the White Lion. Tezuka also introduced the manga tradition of drawing characters with large, round eyes.

Manga's classics, such as *Dragon Ball Z* and *Fullmetal Alchemist*, combine fantasy and science fiction in a fresh way that appeals to readers in America. In fact, American artists are now producing their own manga. Chain bookstores contain manga sections as large as the ones for traditional comics. Makoto Watanabe, professor of media at Hokkaido University, says manga like *Fullmetal Alchemist* are timeless: "You can read them as a child and enjoy the story but go back again much later and find a new story within them."

Quoted in Julian Ryall, "Japan: Manga to Spearhead Nation's Economic Growth," DW, April 23, 2023. www.dw.com.

interested him, with more depth and characterization than before. As a result, Lee and artist Jack Kirby created the Fantastic Four, a team of superheroes who got their superpowers from passing through gamma rays during a spaceflight. Its members quarreled with each other, expressed their fears and anxieties, and dealt with problems from real life. Instead of hiding behind secret identities, they set up their headquarters openly as a superhero group. These fresh ideas spurred Kirby to produce some of his most imaginative art.

The new approach led to a burst of inspiration at Atlas, which changed its name to Marvel Comics. The company launched one hit after another, introducing new characters such as Thor, the Hulk, Iron Man, the X-Men, and Daredevil. Even Captain America returned, having supposedly been frozen in ice since World War II.

But the biggest hit of all emerged from a collaboration between Lee and Steve Ditko, a distinctive journeyman artist. The duo created a teenager who was bitten by a radioactive spider and used his new abilities to become Spider-Man. Unlike the massive musculature of Kirby's heroes, Ditko's Spider-Man looked slender and wiry. He could not fly but instead swung from rooftop to rooftop on webs shot from his wrist shooters. Fans could relate to Peter Parker, the person behind the mask, who had a teenager's romantic problems and often struggled to make ends meet. "[Lee and Ditko] were breaking new ground by making Peter Parker's adolescence the emotional center of their stories," says Ben Saunders, professor of English at the University of Oregon. "When Spider-Man appeared, he expanded the emotional scope of the whole superhero genre."[8] If Superman and Batman were the kings of the golden age of comics, Spider-Man ruled the silver age. And like them, his popularity has never wavered. As of 2021 Spider-Man comics had sold more than 385 million copies.

Underground Comics, Graphic Novels, and Beyond

Another development in comic art had nothing to do with the mainstream comics industry. Underground comics—or *comix*, as

The best-known artist in the underground comics movement was Robert Crumb, who published Zap Comix *and other books. Here, an elderly Crumb looks at a display of some of his work.*

they were often called—drew inspiration from the 1960s counterculture. They sought to expand the boundaries of comic book art with small-press or self-published editions. Ignoring the CCA, underground artists explored themes of sex, drugs, race, violence, and politics with outrageous humor that appealed to a hip young audience. Many of the best underground artists worked in the Mission District of San Francisco, where they swapped ideas and fed on the local rock music, art fads, and literary culture at play.

The best-known artist in the underground movement was Robert Crumb, who published his work in *Zap Comix* and other books as R. Crumb. A talented draftsman, Crumb used the comics format to unpack his own insecurities about sex and race. The results were by turn hilarious and shocking. Crumb relished the absolute freedom to express himself. "I don't like editorial meddling in my work," he wrote years later. "That's why I stick with the 'underground' still."[9]

In the 1970s and 1980s, certain comic artists began to promote longer works as graphic novels with serious artistic intentions. Will Eisner produced one of the first graphic novels, *A Contract with God*, in 1978. By 1982 Marvel Comics had launched its own line of graphic novels. Two celebrated projects in the mid-1980s told superhero stories with a new emotional realism and moral ambiguity. Frank Miller's *The Dark Knight Returns* presented a darker, brooding take on Batman, raising questions about whether he is a crime fighter or a vigilante. English writer Alan Moore's *Watchmen*, drawn by Dave Gibbons, set a group of new superheroes in an alternate-universe America, in which the United States won the Vietnam War and now faces a possible nuclear disaster. These works, first presented as multiple-issue story arcs, were later collected into graphic novel form.

WORDS IN CONTEXT

story arc: A story's plot, from beginning to end

By the 1990s, comics distribution had left drugstore spinner racks behind in favor of specialty stores with direct market sales. "The direct market allowed comic book stores to provide more diversity in the types of comics available to readers," says Ash Chauhan, who writes about popular culture. "The direct market also gave rise to dozens of independent comic book publishers who . . . offered an alternative to readers accustomed to the exploits of costumed heroes that had dominated American comics for the better part of a century."[10] Comics stores stocked current issues, popular back issues, and special editions, as well as all sorts of merchandise connected to comics culture.

Today, despite ups and downs due to the COVID-19 pandemic and changing business models, the comics industry remains robust. In 2021 comic books and graphic novels racked up sales of more than 94 million copies. Sales of digital comics also rose. There are more opportunities for comic book artists, both professionals and amateurs, to self-publish their work. Comic art, in all its various genres and formats, continues to surprise and delight readers around the world.

Chapter Two

Producing Comic Art

Popular superhero comics go back many years, sometimes decades. This can present a challenge for comic book writers and artists, who may struggle to keep up with the continuity, or all the changes and plotlines a character goes through. And eagle-eyed fans are always alert to a slipup. During a video session for *Wired* magazine, artist Todd McFarlane admitted that sometimes he has to adapt and improvise to deal with mistakes in continuity. For his character Spawn, a murdered government agent who is reborn as a demonic vigilante, McFarlane devised an elaborate costume. But readers noticed that details of the costume, the spikes and chains and skulls, would change from issue to issue, even from page to page. Instead of admitting his mistakes, McFarlane hit on the perfect solution. "That's because the costume is alive," he says. "And if anybody ever asks, I go 'Costume's alive, it's always morphing, it's never the same.'"[11] After all, it seemed reasonable for a demon's outfit to be a living parasite—in fact, kind of cool. Eventually, this became a major plot point of the series: Spawn's living suit granted its wearer special powers. As Robert Kirkman, another top comics creator, says, "Sometimes I think fans would be horrified if they knew how much stuff we forget."[12] Both McFarlane and Kirkman admit that producing comics, with the do-or-die stress of deadlines, is bound to be a bit chaotic.

The Basic Tools of Comic Art

Most comic book artists start with the most basic tools of the trade: a pencil and paper. Pencils are chosen according to a graphite scale that uses HB grades to denote lead weight. *H* stands for "hardness" and *B* for "blackness." Today's pencil makers use an HB system with numbers. For example, a 4B is softer than a 2B and produces a thicker, blacker line. And a 3H is harder than an H, producing a finer, lighter line. For comparison, an HB grade in the middle of the scale is roughly equal to the standard number 2 pencil.

Pros note that there is really no *best* pencil for drawing comics. It all depends on what feels comfortable to the user and produces the sort of line desired. Some artists prefer a soft, dark line that smears more easily. Others like a clean line like an etched mark. There is also a choice between typical wooden pencils and lead holders or mechanical pencils, which can be loaded with different types of lead. But aspiring artists should experiment with various pencils until they find what suits them. The *Comic Artist Resource Blog* advises:

> Let's get one thing straight, there is no pencil, pen, marker, drawing table or other random art supply that is going to make you a better artist. The only thing that is going to make you better at drawing comics is practice, practice and oh yeah . . . practice! So don't get caught up in finding the lead and wood equivalent of the Holy Grail, just find some tools you like, stick with them and draw.[13]

Paper is another variable for comic artists. It has different textures, from smooth to rough. Smooth paper enables an artist to emphasize precise details, while rough paper allows for more smearing and shading. Most comic artists use Bristol board paper, which comes in pads of twenty sheets. It is a heavier, oversized paper that absorbs ink and prevents bleeding. It also stands up to erasers—another necessity for beginning artists.

Artist Todd McFarlane, creator of Spawn, *accounted for mistakes in continuity by saying that his character's suit was alive and constantly morphing.*

Inking a finished drawing is what makes it pop out from the page. The black ink not only brings out the lines but also can add shadows, cross-hatching, and feathering for texture. Bottled ink can be applied with nib pens or various kinds of brushes. Waterproof india ink dries without smudging and is best for durability. Many artists also ink their work with fine-point Micron pens, which are precise and inexpensive. Higher-priced Rapidograph pens do the same delicate fine-point work and have refillable cartridges.

WORDS IN CONTEXT

cross-hatching: Intersecting lines for shadows or shading

Drawing can be done on any flat surface. However, most pros work at a drawing board or drafting table. The tilted drawing surface allows the artist to sit upright and work more comfortably. This also

WORDS IN CONTEXT

layout: Arrangement of panels on the page

enables the artist to work longer hours without getting a sore neck or back. Some drafting tables have a built-in glass surface, so that a light under the table creates the effect of a light box. An artist can layer a fresh sheet of paper over a sketch or layout so that the light shines through both sheets, with the bottom image visible. That way a rough sketch or the details of a layout can be traced onto the new sheet.

Tools for Digital Production of Comic Art

Even artists who prefer to create comic art with pencils and pens now often use software programs to aid the process. Among the most frequently used are Adobe Illustrator and Adobe Photoshop. Illustrator helps letterers produce cover logos, fonts, sound effects, and dialogue balloons. Photoshop is even more useful for its ability to clean up mistakes on scans, insert changes to artwork without redrawing, and rapidly add all sorts of visual effects, such as lighting and coloring.

An exciting all-in-one digital tool specifically designed for producing comics is called Clip Studio Paint. It speeds up the drawing process with tools like the perspective ruler, which sets the vanishing points in an illustration and then snaps the lines into place on a grid. This is extremely useful for backgrounds and complicated cityscapes. Clip Studio Paint also helps with coloring line drawings consistently across an entire story without Photoshop. Dave Gibbons, the award-winning cocreator of the classic *Watchmen* comic book series, was an early adopter of software for comic artwork, and he swears by Clip Studio Paint. "First, I love the tools," he says. "I love how closely they emulate and imitate real world tools. I have my toolbox set up to use the digital equivalents of exactly the tools I had come to use in the analog world. I just love the responsiveness you get from the pencils, pens, and brushes."[14] For professionals and amateurs alike, Clip Studio Paint can be a game changer for digital comics production.

Creating the Layout and Breakdowns

With tools at hand, an artist is ready to start creating a comic story. The starting point for a comics page is the layout. This is the arrangement of panels on the page, selected as being the best way to tell the story. A layout may be as simple as thumbnails on a sheet of notepaper or as elaborate as a full-size mock-up. Panels have space between them, called the gutter, that helps keep them separate visually. It is important that the reader's eye can easily follow the action from the top left panel to the bottom right panel. Yet the layout of panels need not be a regular row of squares or rectangles. Panels can be different shapes and sizes to emphasize what is happening. An action sequence may have larger panels for more impact, while a dialogue scene may have smaller panels. One or more panels may be insets, which means they are set inside a larger panel.

Comic artist Steve Ellis sometimes tries to create even more of a feeling of speed or urgency. "If I am looking to lead the reader from one picture to another or give the feeling that one or more panels are happening either simultaneously or directly after, I

Finding the Right Eraser

Comic artists who do pencil drawings tend to rely on their erasers. These tools of the trade can help fix big mistakes and delicately remove tiny errors. "While I could draw without erasers, my drawing technique would be tremendously different without them," says Carol Rosinski of Toad Hollow Studio. "I depend on my erasers as much as I depend on my pencils, so I guess I'm officially a pencil *and* eraser artist."

A kneaded rubber eraser is an essential tool for comic artists. Its soft composition allows it to be pinched and molded into precise shapes for tricky erasing jobs. It will lift graphite away with a light press, so that harsh rubbing (and torn paper) is not necessary. Kneaded erasers also work well for cleaning up the outer edges of a drawing or removing smeared areas.

A soft, nonabrasive block eraser is more of a standard tool and works well with 2B pencil lead. Hi-polymer eraser caps, like the ones on pencils in grade school, also are effective without damaging the page. An erasing shield is another helpful tool for precise erasing. Artists can place the shield on the drawing so that only the lines or line segments they want to remove are exposed.

Carol Rosinski, "The Best Erasers for Graphite Pencil Drawing," Carol's Drawing Blog, 2023. www.toadhollowstudio.com.

will overlap panels," says Ellis. "But it's a difficult trick because you need to make sure that elements of one panel don't bleed into another panel making it hard to separate the beats of the page."[15] The artist also has to decide where the scene-setting captions and dialogue balloons will go. The placement of dialogue balloons helps the reader tell which character is speaking and in what order.

WORDS IN CONTEXT

breakdowns: Rough sketches of what each panel should contain

Next comes the breakdowns of the story. Breakdowns are the preliminary pencil work in a layout. They include rough sketches of what each panel should contain, such as the basic position for each character. Artists generally recommend keeping the action flowing from left to right. This leads the reader's eye across the page. Breakdowns are also where the artist begins to plot the action like a movie director. The panels can present different perspectives for emotional effect, such as aerial views, low-level viewpoints, wide-angle panoramas, or character close-ups. The breakdown might help the artist plan a dramatic reveal. Artist Jack Kirby liked to set up a sequence of smaller pan-

Many artists ink their work with fine-point Micron pens, which are precise and inexpensive. Higher-priced Rapidograph pens, pictured, do the same delicate fine-point work and have refillable cartridges.

The Controversial Inker

Many comic book inkers are talented artists in their own right, and their inking is done with an artistic flair. But what looks acceptable might actually be part sabotage. Comic book fans often point to the inking that Vince Colletta did for Jack Kirby's pencil work in the 1950s and 1960s. Upon first inspection it looks fine, displaying Colletta's light touch and feathery details. But by comparing Colletta's inked drawings to Kirby's penciled originals, it is obvious that Colletta left out details and sometimes whole figures.

It turns out that Colletta was notorious for working fast and loose. Comics blogger Tom Brevoort says:

> Colletta had a work ethic that said that he needed to complete a certain amount of work every day in order to finance his lifestyle, and that's what he did, regardless of what he needed to do to accomplish that goal. He was a favorite of editors, especially when a story was in trouble schedule-wise. Vinnie could always be depended upon to get the job done lickety-split, and nobody was all that concerned with how much may have been lost in translation so long as the presses could roll.

One wonders whether Kirby, a fast worker himself, knew about this—or even cared.

Tom Brevoort, "The Unknown Vince Colletta," *The Tom Brevoort Experience*, January 3, 2021. https://tombrevoort.com.

els at the bottom of a right-hand page leading to a full-page panel (called a splash panel) when the reader turned the page.

In doing the layout and breakdowns, an artist may work from a complete detailed script or an outline. Some writers describe what they expect to see in each panel, while others leave those decisions to the artist. A number of comic artists do both the writing and penciling. This gives them a better opportunity to create their own vision of the story.

Finishing the Pages

Once the layout and breakdowns are complete, the artist does the final drawings in pencil for each page. Most artists start with light, sketchy lines and then add darker lines as the drawing is worked into final shape. An artist may take anywhere from several hours to several days to complete one page of comic book art. The incentive is to work fast in order to meet deadlines and earn more money overall.

Next comes the inker, who uses a pen or brush to draw over the penciller's lines in black ink. This creates a cleaner, bolder, more defined final image. Inking adds shadows, cross-hatchings, stippling, and other details. Expert inkers are sometimes called embellishers for the way they bring out the strongest qualities in a drawing. Comparing the grayscale look of an original pencil-drawn page with the vivid, black-and-white inked version shows the influence of a talented inker. "Another crucial aspect of inking in comic art is its role in the printing process," say the editors at the website ComicBookPros. "Inking ensures that the final comic looks as good on paper as it does on the artist's page. The lines must be clean and crisp, allowing for clear reproduction and legibility."[16]

Breakdowns are the preliminary pencil work in a layout. Artists do breakdowns of a story that include rough sketches of what each panel should contain.

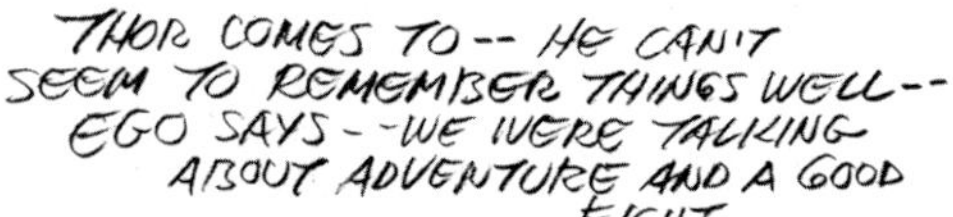

THOR SAYS YES -- I SENSE DANGER APPROACHING -- EGO SAYS THAT'S MORE LIKE IT--

The colorist applies color to the page. This step can be more complex than it appears at first. A good colorist can vary the page's emotional impact by varying the shades, adding highlights, or washing whole panels or a series of panels in one color, like a vivid red or melancholy blue. Often, this step is done digitally, to ensure that the colors are added with no gaps.

A letterer fills in the caption boxes and the dialogue balloons. Captions tell the setting or time for a scene. They may also provide a narrator's commentary on the action. Dialogue balloons contain the characters' spoken words and are layered to show the sequence of a conversation. Cloud bubbles may also be used to display a character's thoughts. Superhero comics would not be complete without sound effects in large block letters (WHOOM!!).

The Printing Process

A printing company handles all the details of printing comic books. It offers choices for paper, covers, and bindings. Comic book art files can also be submitted to an online printing company as a pdf file. The company can use the individual files to produce the physical comic books. It is important to request a proof copy to check for errors and make sure the book looks exactly as expected.

Online or digital comics enable an independent comic artist to publish work without going through the printing process. There's no right answer when comparing paperbound comic books and digital comics. It just depends on which kind artists prefer or which they can live with. "Physical comics are definitely for people who appreciate touch," says comic book aficionado David Harth. "There's also nothing like the new comic smell, or even just the smell of a comic store in general, a pulpy aroma of paper and ink."[17] Longtime collectors like Harth believe it is unlikely that comics on paper will disappear anytime soon.

Skills and Career Paths for Comic Artists

A large publisher introduces a major new comic about an urban couple facing a sudden pandemic of zombie-ism and zombie attacks. The publisher also introduces a new superhero comic, *Sprocketman*, about a costumed figure who fights crime while focusing on bicycle safety. A third title, *The 9 Lives of El Gato the Cat*, follows the adventures of a cat heavily into fire prevention. What comic artist would not be interested in jumping on board and developing these characters and story lines?

The publisher of these titles is not one of the usual comic book companies. It is actually the US government, working through agencies such as the Centers for Disease Control and Prevention and the Consumer Product Safety Commission. The government sponsors these comic book efforts to reach a targeted audience with stories that cross barriers of language and education. The comics can also educate citizens about how to respond to an emergency. The zombie comic, called *Preparedness 101: Zombie Pandemic*, uses the story of a zombie apocalypse to relate how citizens and government scientists would react to a viral pandemic. Distributed to schools and civic groups, *Zombie Pandemic* covered many of the issues that became deadly serious during the COVID-19 pandemic. With Bob Hobbs's macabre artwork and writer Maggie Silver's touches of humor, *Zombie Pandemic* tells a gripping story while also delivering tips on how to prepare for a widespread medical emergency. A note at the end says, "We hope you enjoyed reading this fictional story. . . . Now that you've seen the importance of being prepared, take the time to put together an emergency kit with the items included in the checklist on the following page. You'll be ready for any kind of disaster, even zombies."[18] *Preparedness 101: Zombie Pandemic* shows the opportunities available to comic artists, even outside the comics industry.

Essential Skills for a Comic Artist

Whatever one's career path in comic art, the essential skill is being able to draw. That means drawing recognizable people, objects, and backgrounds from many different perspectives. Drawing styles may vary, from simple to complex. But comics are not the genre for abstract art. It is helpful to earn an art school degree in drawing and graphic design. Many art schools offer programs that specialize in comic book art, web comics, and graphic novels.

To develop professional skills, aspiring comic artists should practice drawing people at every opportunity. Having a sketch pad and pencil nearby should become second nature. It helps to experiment with all kinds of body positions, facial features, and facial expressions. Some artists practice drawing figures from life that they see in the park or on the sidewalk. In the studio, artists can refer to wooden posing figures when drawing different body positions. There are even wooden mannequin hands that can be adjusted for drawing hand and finger positions. A comic artist should also learn how to group figures in dramatic arrangements so that they overlap and interact.

Software such as Clip Studio Paint helps with digital figure drawing using three-dimensional models much like the wooden posing figures. "Understanding figure drawing is absolutely relevant to cartoon art in my opinion," says Krishna Sadasivam, a professional cartoon and comic artist. "A good understanding of anatomy is necessary to convey a sense of believability in the

To develop their professional skills, aspiring comic artists should take every opportunity to practice drawing people. Artists need to experiment with different body positions as well as various facial features and expressions.

character. It's also vital to understand with regards to capturing the character in various poses."[19]

It can take years of practice and experimentation for a comic artist to develop a personal style. Along the way, there is nothing wrong with borrowing things from favorite comic artists. Even the best pros do it. "Jack Kirby's storytelling. John Byrne for his action," says Todd McFarlane, describing his influences. "When Gil Kane [characters] hit somebody it felt like you were getting shot out of a cannon. George Pérez could draw machinery that stuns me. Marshall Rogers did some of the coolest capes. All these blend to make my style."[20] On this point Sadasivam is in full agreement. "Use copying as a method to understand how an artist conveys form, rhythm and visual appeal," he says. "Study the artists that you like. Steal the techniques you like from each and every one of them."[21]

A fully developed, identifiable style makes an artist's work more marketable. A personal style or brand is even more important if your goal is to freelance or work independently. Professionals recommend that new artists compile an ongoing portfolio with ten to

WORDS IN CONTEXT

portfolio: A collection of samples of an artist's work

fifteen of their best, most characteristic drawings. A portfolio should focus on the kind of work you want to do. If you want to draw comic books, include samples of full pages with panels, not pinup pictures. Include samples showing the full range of your abilities, from facial expressions to body positions. It also helps to include samples of street scenes with details of power lines, traffic lights, automobiles, alleyways, and fire escapes. The portfolio is the aspiring pro's calling card, designed to impress an editor. Artists can also post samples of their work on sites such as LinkedIn, Upwork, and Guru.

A Talent for Storyboarding

Along with drawing skill, a comic artist must have the instincts of a movie director. It is often pointed out that a comic book page is much like the storyboard of a film. Like a director, the comic artist

The Comic Artist's Professional Hazard: Deadlines

Comic artists must learn to deal with one of the profession's recurring headaches, which is deadline pressure. For comic book creators, a schedule is generally set upon signing a contract. The artist must produce a certain number of pages in a set amount of time, without delays. Other artists—inkers, colorists, and letterers—depend on the artists' ability to meet deadlines to keep up with their own work. Failure to meet deadlines can be disastrous. "I've worked with experienced artists who have delivered their pages up to six weeks late," says Martin Shapiro, a comic book writer and screenwriter, "which caused the book to miss the printer deadline and delayed the release of the book to comic stores by over one full month. . . . This turned off customers who had previously purchased issue #1 and expected a monthly book series."

Deadline pressure can even derail careers. Bill Watterson, whose *Calvin and Hobbes* strip was one of the greatest and most popular ever, reached a point that deadline pressure was ruling his life to an intolerable degree. Rather than let the quality of his work decline, Watterson, only thirty-seven at the time, decided to retire from the drawing board for good in 1995.

Martin Shapiro, "Deadlines and Flaky Artists," Thunderstruck, May 28, 2022. https://thunderstruckpictures.co.

WORDS IN CONTEXT

silhouettes: Outlines of people or things filled in with black or another color

plans the most effective way to tell a story and convey emotion to the reader. This is done by varying the point of view and mixing in long shots, medium shots, groupings of characters, aerial views, silhouettes, and close-ups. Shadows and moody coloring also add to the emotional content. A talented artist can present a shattering climax without words. For example, a tragic scene might focus on the changing facial reaction of a single character in a sequence of panels down the page.

Some artists—such as Michelle Lam, Aaron Sowd, and Trevor Goring—use their storyboarding talents to find success both in comics and film. For example, Sowd has developed comics for both DC and Marvel as well as doing storyboards for film directors like Steven Soderbergh. Goring has split time between comics work and superhero film projects like *Watchmen* and *X-Men*. "With comics, you're the director, production designer, fashion designer, etc., rolled into one," says Goring. "You usually have more time; you can be more nuanced because in a film the director needs to be able to see instantly what's going on in the frame. In a comic the reader can take more time looking at panels."[22]

Opportunities in the Comic Book Industry

Versatile comic artists have more career opportunities in the comics field than ever before. Although sales figures in the industry go up and down, in the past decade they have trended solidly higher on average. The slump in 2020, the first year of the COVID-19 pandemic, was followed by 48 percent higher sales in 2021 and record revenues of $2.07 billion. This represented sales of 94 million copies of comic books and graphic novels in the United States. From 2012 through 2021, comic book sales generated more than $11.4 billion.

The giants of the industry, Marvel and DC, continue to dominate sales. Since 2011 they have combined to produce more than two-thirds of total sales revenue for comic books. Nonetheless,

A comic book page is much like a storyboard for a film. Like a movie director, the artist plans the most effective way to tell a story and convey emotion to the reader.

the smaller independents—including Image Comics, Dark Horse Comics, and IDW Publishing—have managed to achieve at least 15 percent of overall annual sales. These companies are often more welcoming to novice artists and new characters whose quirkiness is their main appeal. And the smaller companies still offer the chance of adaptation to other media. Image's *The Walking Dead*, a postapocalyptic zombie saga by writer Robert Kirkman and artist Tony Moore, became a long-running TV series on AMC starting in 2010. It has also spawned a couple of spin-offs, a fan-centered show (*Talking Dead*), video games, and millions of dollars in merchandising.

Page Rates and Royalties

Only a few comic artists work on a salaried basis, according to an income survey from Creator Resource. Most artists are paid by the project, receiving an agreed-upon amount for the finished book. This amount breaks down into page rates, or payment

WORDS IN CONTEXT

royalties: Money paid to an artist based on sales of a comic

per page. Pencillers at DC and Marvel, for example, receive about $200 per page. Thus, penciling a 20-page comic book for one of the leading companies would earn the artist around $4,000. Cover art, which tends to be elaborate, pays about $800.

Companies sometimes sweeten the contract with royalty rates based on sales. The rates vary wildly, from 10 percent to 80 percent, and the deals may include deductions for printing and shipping costs. Royalty payments are based on sales, giving the artist a major incentive to do innovative work that attracts a large audience.

Comic artists have another option, which is to own their own creations. For a flat fee, Image Comics will publish a creator's comic book, giving the artist access to distribution in comics stores. That way the artist's financial success (or failure) will depend entirely on the marketplace.

Targeting an Artist's Work in *Hawkeye*

A major issue for comic artists is getting paid when their work is adapted for another medium. In 2021 fans awaiting the premier of Marvel's new TV series *Hawkeye* noticed something familiar about the promotional art. Posters of the archer hero Hawkeye aiming an arrow at the viewer were very similar to ads for a Hawkeye comic book series in 2012. The TV promotion also featured purple arrow-shaped graphics and archery targets with the same distinctive look as the comic book ads. When the series finally debuted in November 2021, fans discovered that the graphics for the show's opening and closing credits drew heavily on the comics' artwork. The series also featured new characters created for the comics, including a lovable golden retriever named Lucky the Pizza Dog. Yet David Aja, a Spanish artist who did the stylish drawings for the *Hawkeye* comics, was not mentioned in the credits.

Outraged fans took to social media with threats to boycott the TV series. Most of the posts demanded that Aja receive on-screen credit for his artwork. But Aja himself followed up with his own take on Twitter: "Even better: Stop crediting, start paying, haha." To head off the brewing controversy, Marvel Studios announced it would pay Aja an undisclosed amount.

Quoted in Math Erao, "*Hawkeye* Artist David Aja Calls Out Marvel Studios for Not Paying for Adapted Work," CBR, October 27, 2021. www.cbr.com.

Comic book artists can profit when their work is adapted to other media. For example, Image Comics' The Walking Dead *(shown here) became a long-running television series.*

Web Comics for Pros and Amateurs

There are also opportunities in web comics, or comics published on a mobile app or website. The market for web comics is surprisingly large and growing, earning $7.36 billion in 2021. Some artists use web comics mostly as a promotional tool to attract other work. But an increasing number are making a living from web comics through subscriptions, advertising, and merchandising. Platforms that offer subscription services for web comics include Patreon, Ko-fi, and Buy Me a Coffee. Popular web comics can bring in merchandise sales of coffee cups, T-shirts, greeting cards, posters, and stickers. One genre that has drawn particular interest is romance. Both male and female readers have flocked to read web comics like *Lore Olympus*, a modern retelling of a Greek myth, or *Check Please!*, a quirky story about love, hockey, and baking pies.

Artists can create a new kind of web comic on a site called Webtoon. A webtoon is a digital comic form, similar to manga, that originated in South Korea. Its stories, in twenty-three genres, are usually intended to be read quickly by scrolling down on a smartphone. Some see webtoons' popularity among youths as part of South Korea's so-called snack culture. "This refers to the modern consumer's demand for bite-sized entertainment that can be consumed in 15 minutes or less," says Alisha Christina Moffat, a writer on the How to Love Comics website. "This makes webtoons even more accessible by catering to both today's average attention span and our constantly busy lifestyles."[23] The Webtoons platform hosts hundreds of artists' work, ranging from amateurs who are able to publish for free to pros who adapt their comic book work to the format, as in DC Comics' *Batman: Wayne Family Adventures*.

Amateur artists intent on getting their work seen can also post their comics on social media, especially Facebook and Instagram. Posting one or two pages a week to friends keeps them invested in the story and waiting for the next plot twist.

More Options than Ever Before

Becoming a comic artist calls for long hours of practice drawing every kind of human figure, body position, and facial expression. An artist should think of the job as similar to that of a film director or cinematographer, choosing shots and angles for their storytelling effect and emotional content. Once the necessary skill set is developed, a comic artist has to decide whether to seek a career at a comics company or pursue the trade as an independent contractor. With new formats appearing all the time, comic artists have more options than ever before for marketing their work. "We live in an ever-changing world of digital technology, and it seems like there are always new ways of creating your artwork and getting it seen by more and more fans," wrote Marvel's legendary Stan Lee. "And no doubt the ways that people will read your work will continue to change with it."[24]

The Giants of Comic Art, Past and Present

In the Prints and Photographs division of the Library of Congress, comic book fans take selfies of themselves alongside some yellowing pages. The pages contain the original artwork for an old comic, *Amazing Fantasy* #15. The title page is filled with Wite-Out blotches, tape, and half-erased editorial comments. Fancy web-design letters have been covered over with more traditional block letters. For this origin story, the details had to be just right. One demand is to add a hyphen to the main character's name: Spider-Man.

The Library of Congress is a high-class neighborhood for these old pages drawn by artist Steve Ditko. Adding to their mysterious appeal, curator Sara W. Duke refuses to divulge the name of their donor or how that person obtained them in the first place. To her, all of that is a distraction. "Isn't it great that it ended up in an archive, rather than some wealthy person's basement, where they don't take it out of the box?" says Duke. "Now, anybody can come and enjoy it. That, to me, is the epitome of generosity."[25] At any rate, the library preserves the pages like precious relics. To view them, visitors must be sixteen or older and have a government-issued ID. Close examination of the pages shows that Ditko, a prickly, independent sort, ignored most of editor Stan Lee's suggestions for changes. As Duke notes, "In this case, you had two headstrong creators who both said [Spider-Man] was their idea—you have direct evidence of that collaborative nature of that production."[26] Perhaps more original artwork from the 1960s Marvel studio will turn up in the future. For now, the growing interest in original comic artwork, and the high prices it can bring at auction, shows how the greatest creators of comic art have staked their place in American culture.

The King of Comics

To baby boomers awash in nostalgia, certain comic artists are like royalty. Their instantly recognizable styles bring back that delicious thrill of excitement when a new batch of comic books would appear on the dime-store spinner racks. However, one name nearly always ranks at the top: Jack "King" Kirby.

Born Jacob Kurtzberg in 1917, Kirby grew up in the tough Lower East Side neighborhood of Hell's Kitchen in New York City. He loved to draw and was self-taught, learning his trade by studying the work of popular comic strip artists such as Hal Foster on *Prince Valiant* and Alex Raymond on *Flash Gordon*. One of his first jobs was drawing cartoon cells for Max Fleischer's animation studio. Early in 1941 the publisher Martin Goodman approached Kirby and his studio partner, Joe Simon, with an offer to create new characters for his comics business. Bursting with ideas and ambition, the pair quickly developed Captain America, a patriotic superhero who gained extraordinary strength and agility from a government super-soldier experiment. The cover of *Captain America* #1 won over young readers with its image of Cap punching Nazi leader Adolf Hitler on the jaw. The first printing sold out within a week.

Although raw compared to his mature style, Kirby's early artwork seemed to jump off the page. His animation experience taught him how to express action, with dynamic figures sprinting, leaping, and lunging outside of the panels. But Kirby and Simon soon got into disputes with Goodman over stingy payment rates. They moved on, first to DC Comics, and then to other companies. Kirby learned early the benefits of being versatile as an artist. It helped

The Prints and Photographs division of the Library of Congress displays original artwork of comics such as Amazing Fantasy's introduction of Spider-Man.

him keep busy doing whatever genre of comic was popular at the time, whether war comics, crime, romance, or giant monsters.

By the late 1950s Kirby had split with Simon and taken a job with Stan Lee at what would become Marvel Comics. Together with Lee, Kirby created the Fantastic Four, made up of four superheroes with different powers and personalities. The Thing, a bitter, orange, rocklike monster who longed to be human again, spoke in New York slang, puffed on cigars, and generally reminded Marvel's other artists of Kirby himself. Critics disagree about who came up with what between Lee and Kirby, but no one could deny the quality of their creations in the *Fantastic Four* series: Dr. Doom, the Silver Surfer, the Inhumans, the Black Panther, and many more. Kirby also helped create and develop a who's who of other Marvel superheroes, including the Hulk, Thor, Iron Man, the X-Men, and the Avengers. Along the way, he designed wondrously futuristic machinery for his stories and invented graphic effects like the so-called Kirby dots or Kirby Krackle—black dots that gave the effect of raw energy sizzling to life. Plus, he worked with extraordinary speed, completing at least five pages a day.

Kirby's classic stint with Marvel lasted barely more than a decade. He was chronically overworked, underpaid, and in search

Meeting the Star Artists at Comic-Con

In 1969, comics fan Sheldon Dorf decided to organize a fan convention in his new hometown of San Diego, California. To give the idea some extra oomph, Dorf called his favorite artist, Jack Kirby, who lived in Irvine. Kirby not only agreed to appear at the first convention, he drew the cover for its program. Beginning with one hundred fans in the basement of an old downtown hotel, the convention grew steadily from year to year.

Now the most prestigious event of its kind, San Diego Comic-Con regularly features the biggest names among comic artists in the industry. Fans get autographs, purchase art and merchandise, and attend panel discussions about how comics are produced. For comic artists who labor alone, it is a chance to get the star treatment and find out personally how much their work means to fans. The convention has also expanded to include Hollywood actors and writers from comic book and science-fiction films as well as animation pros and video game creators. Fans also indulge in cosplay, dressing up as their favorite comic characters. As Joe Allen reports for the website Digital Trends, "At its core, Comic-Con is all about finding ways for the people behind nerd culture to connect with the genre's many fans."

Joe Allen, "The Best San Diego Comic-Con Panels Ever," Digital Trends, July 19, 2023. www.digitaltrends.com.

of a better working arrangement at other publishers. He spent his last years wrangling with Marvel over his penciled art pages, which were often given away to company clients or stolen from the warehouse. Kirby died in 1994, years before his creations reached a new level of fame—and billions in value—on movie screens worldwide. According to Randolph Hoppe, acting executive director of the Jack Kirby Museum & Research Center, "Kirby could sit down at a drawing board with a pencil and some 2-ply Bristol board and, within hours or days, finish a multi-page dramatic tale of cosmic war, heartfelt romance or criminal justice. . . . His goal was to pull his readers in, make them feel that they were *in* the story, the outside world peeling away, as if they were in a theater watching a movie."[27]

Eisner and the Spirit Section

One of Kirby's key influences was Will Eisner. Eisner was born in Brooklyn, New York, in 1917. In 1940 he launched a new character, the Spirit, in a seven-page comic book included as a supplement in Sunday newspapers across the nation. The Spirit Section, as it was called, featured a story starring either the masked crime fighter or some related character. Inventive by nature, Eisner used all his resources as an artist to make the Spirit's adventures unique. He loved to end his stories with a surprise twist. But his most famous innovation was the full-page splash panel that introduced each Spirit Section. It might be a mock-up of a newspaper front page with the headline "THE SPIRIT! WHO IS HE?"[28] It might show a haunted house with the logo of the Spirit built into the entranceway with cobwebs. A celebrated story called "The Elevator" began with an aerial shot of tall, narrow industrial buildings that spelled out the hero's name.

Eisner let his imagination run wild all through these Sunday gems. "The work was uniquely comics, existing in the place where the words and the pictures come together," wrote comic writer Neil Gaiman on the one-hundredth anniversary of Eisner's birth. "Eisner's stories were influenced by film, by theatre, by radio, but were ultimately their own medium, created by a man who thought that comics was an artform, and who was proved right."[29]

Gaiman, assisted by artist Dave McKean, used Eisner's work as inspiration for his own breakthrough comic series, *Sandman*. Rejecting the usual comic book battle scenes, Gaiman and McKean devised a cover for each issue that expressed the series' idea of a dreamworld in paintings, drawings, blurred photocopies, or collage. *Sandman* appeared in the mid-1990s when the comics industry was in a slump, but it ended up outselling DC's flagship *Batman* and *Superman* comics. Gaiman also ended up starting another trend in the industry. When his run on *Sandman* came to an end, DC canceled the title instead of passing it on to another creative team. Despite its history of large sales, DC editor Karen Berger agreed that no one could replace Gaiman and McKean.

WORDS IN CONTEXT

flagship: The best or most important item or items in a group

A Graphic Novel from the Underground

Sandman, *Watchmen*, *Batman: Year One*, and other ambitious comic book arcs continued the push to view comics as serious graphic novels. (In fact, it was Eisner who coined the term *graphic novel*.) One of the most celebrated graphic novels came from an artist who started his career in San Francisco's underground comics scene in the late 1960s and early 1970s. In 1972 Art Spiegelman began work on an experimental, autobiographical comic based on his relationship with his father, who had survived a Nazi death camp. Over the years the new work swelled to three hundred pages. The result was *Maus: A Survivor's Tale*, an allegory of the Holocaust in which cats are Nazis, mice are Jews, and pigs are ethnic Poles.

WORDS IN CONTEXT

allegory: A story told by means of symbolic figures

The work of comic book artist Jack Kirby is celebrated in a 2015 exhibition. Kirby was co-creator of many beloved Marvel superheroes including the Hulk, Thor, Iron Man, the X-Men, and the Avengers.

Reviewers found the book to be remarkably powerful. In 1992 *Maus* was awarded a special Pulitzer Prize. Spiegelman attributes the book's impact to his years drawing underground comics and sharing ideas with like-minded artists out to do something fresh and innovative. "For me to be able to bring the vocabulary of everything from Gertrude Stein and James Joyce to Picasso and other more formal aspects of picture-making, opened up very new territory," he says. "In order to do 'Maus,' everything I learned here became new vocabulary for me."[30]

Diverse Figures in Comic Art

Today's comics industry features many more Black, Latino, and female artists than ever before. Yet even in the golden age, standout minority artists found ways to make their mark. In 1945 African American artist Matt Baker created Voodah, the first Black character in a White comic book. Baker had noticed that all the Africa-based jungle characters in comics, both heroes and heroines, were unaccountably White. So with Voodah, Baker introduced a dark-skinned jungle hero ready to rescue innocents in danger. Baker later became famous for his renderings of voluptuous female characters, including Phantom Lady, a scantily clad crime fighter.

Queens, New York–born Kyle Baker is one of the most respected Black comic artists and animators today. Starting out as an inker with Marvel Comics, Baker (no relation to Matt Baker) soon graduated to doing his own books. In 1990 he won the prestigious Eisner Award for his graphic novel *Why I Hate Saturn*. He later had a successful run with his reboot of the golden age hero Plastic Man.

Marie Severin was a trailblazing female artist for the 1950s EC horror comics. Later, at Marvel, she took over the Dr. Strange feature from Steve Ditko and ended up winning awards for her imaginative work. As more female artists today have found suc-

A Milestone in Comic Art

By the mid-1980s, artists and writers would take over superhero comics for short runs, putting their own spin on a popular character. British writer Alan Moore swooped into DC Comics and demonstrated his chops by revitalizing the creepy character Swamp Thing, whose book was about to be canceled. Next, Moore intended to pump some life into a collection of obscure superheroes that DC had obtained from failing publisher Charlton Comics. Instead, he used the Charlton characters as templates for new heroes and set them in an alternate universe.

The twelve-issue run was called *Watchmen*, from a Latin quote that translates to "Who watches the watchmen?" Moore and artist Dave Gibbons created a world on the brink of nuclear disaster, where superheroes are regarded more as vigilantes than saviors. The team wove a complicated plot that included a murder mystery and shocking character revelations. Their heroes—including Doctor Manhattan, Rorschach, and Nite Owl—battled their own personal demons while trying to avert a catastrophe. Like a complex novel, *Watchmen* scatters subtle details at the beginning that prove to be decisive in the end. "It's way beyond cliché at this point to call *Watchmen* the greatest superhero comic ever written-slash-drawn," says *Time* magazine. "But it's true."

Lev Grossman, "Top 10 Graphic Novels: *Watchmen*," *Time*, March 4, 2009. https://time.com.

One of the most celebrated graphic novels is Art Spiegelman's Maus: A Survivor's Tale, *an allegory of the Holocaust, in which cats are Nazis, mice are Jews, and pigs are ethnic Poles.*

cess in the comics field, some have seized the opportunity to slip social commentary into their comic stories. Joëlle Jones, who has worked on *Vampirella* and *Catwoman* comics, is best known for her 2015 *Lady Killer* series for Dark Horse Comics. In *Lady Killer*, her staid, old-fashioned scenes of domestic peace tend to suddenly burst into shocking violence. Mariko Tamaki's *She-Hulk: Deconstructed* focused on female rage and strength while also showing the lawyer character's acute intelligence.

Among the most accomplished Latino artists is Puerto Rico–born George Pérez. In 1975 Pérez introduced Marvel's first Latino hero, Hector Ayala, also known as White Tiger. He worked on the celebrated Thanos–*Infinity Gauntlet* series that became the basis for several films in the Marvel Cinematic Universe.

Rising Talents

Today a whole new crop of comic artists is carrying on the imaginative work of the golden and silver age pioneers. DC artists such as Jorge Jiménez, Clay Mann, and Matteo Scalera have all brought a new perspective on Batman and other classic characters. Laura Braga has playfully combined the worlds of DC and *Archie Comics* in *Harley & Ivy Meet Betty & Veronica*. Federica Mancin is a young artist who is channeling Marvel's classic legacy in her work on Spider-Man and his Afro-Latino alter ego, Miles Morales. "Having the opportunity to work on a Miles Morales issue as my first job at Marvel has been a dream come true as he is my favorite Marvel character," she says. "Of course, all the action sequences were super fun to me, as I love trying to find ways to convey energy and motion through the page."[31] King Kirby could hardly have said it better himself.

WORDS IN CONTEXT

alter ego: A person's second or alternate personality

Chapter Five

The Future of Comic Art

In the comic book *Zarya of the Dawn*, the title character travels to different worlds to garner tools for mental health, tools that will help in handling strong emotions. But the book itself has sparked strong reactions among legal experts and comic book artists. New York author Kristina Kashtanova wrote the texts for *Zarya*. However, the art was produced entirely by the AI program Midjourney. When Kashtanova sought to copyright her work, she ran into legal obstacles from the US Copyright Office (USCO). In February 2023, following a monthlong review, the USCO ruled that the text of the book and the arrangement of images would remain in copyright but that the AI-generated images themselves would have no such protection. Kashtanova, who works as a consultant at a New York tech company that deals in AI, protested that she had written the prompts for *Zarya*'s art herself. "It is fundamental to understand that the output of a Generative AI depends directly on the creative input of the artist and is not random,"[32] she posted on social media.

One month later, the USCO amended its ruling, if only slightly. It said that future AI-created comics might receive different levels of copyright protection depending on what AI tools were used in their creation. In general, however, authors could not copyright a character's AI-generated appearance or costume. Nonetheless, Van Lindberg, Kashtanova's lawyer, remains optimistic about the future of AI in comics. "I think the USCO will need to adopt a wider embrace of AI-assisted content," says Lindberg. "There is too much creative activity occurring using AI tools for that to be . . . the final conclusion."[33]

Controversy over AI-Generated Comics

AI technology has arrived just as the comic book industry is facing new questions about its future. Although overall sales have bounced back from the COVID-19 slump, questions remain about whether printed comic books are still viable. Fees for comic book artists have been falling, and some independent publishers have missed payments to freelancers and even considered filing for bankruptcy.

WORDS IN CONTEXT

freelancers: Artists who work independently and are paid on a per-job basis

In the face of these challenges, some see AI as a potential savior. A rising generation of tech-savvy comic creators have no problem turning to AI art generators such as Midjourney, Stable Diffusion, and DALL-E for assistance. Some welcome the technology as a needed jolt to an industry they see as having grown stale and predictable. And AI does hold out intriguing possibilities. "With AI, creators can instantly generate a wide variety of images or artwork by simply describing them through words," says tech analyst and comic book fan Evan Ezquer. "These generated images can then be used to create characters, panels, covers, and virtually every visual aspect of a comic book."[34]

Some supporters say AI is democratizing the art form and will lead to new levels of creativity. They compare use of AI to tools like Photoshop, which also manipulate digital images according to a user's instructions. They say producing comics, which has long been a collaborative process among several people—including writers, artists, inkers, colorists, and letterers—can now be accomplished by an individual with a major assist from AI. Supporters worry that the USCO's decision limiting copyright for AI-generated comics could slow the technology's adoption. Artists might hesitate to experiment with AI for fear of losing the rights to what they create.

A rising cadre of tech-savvy comic creators are turning to AI art generators such as DALL-E for assistance in making images.

Opposition to AI-generated comics has been heated. It has come from both longtime industry professionals and comic fans. Pros object that AI performs work that should go to flesh-and-blood artists. They also level charges of plagiarism, pointing out that AI uses published artwork from online data sets in producing its images, without compensating its creators. Many comic editors have admitted they are biased against any submission in which AI was used. As for fans, many are expressing fears that AI-generated comics replace human creativity with cold algorithms. Moreover, they love the individual stylistic tics of their favorite artists, which spark endless debates about who is best at what. Fans would hate to see this kind of passionate response to artistic styles become a moot point with AI.

WORDS IN CONTEXT

plagiarism: Copying or using someone else's work without crediting them

Enabling Amateurs and Nonartists to Create Comics

Supporters of AI technology point out that it enables amateurs and nonartists to make their own comics. With AI, a person need not have any talent for drawing to create an interesting—and beautifully rendered—comic book. What is needed instead are fresh ideas about plot, character, and setting and the ability to write precise prompts that tell the program exactly what the artist wants. Even with precise instructions, AI is likely to startle its user with the professional-looking comic pages that are generated in full color. Some programs also include dialogue balloons, although they generally are filled with gibberish and meant to make the panels look more like a genuine comic.

AI offers other selling points for creators, whether amateur or professional. It greatly reduces the cost of creating a comic book, which can range from $140 to $200 a page and more than $5,000

Concerns About the Future of Comics

When asked if the traditional comic book has a future, Bob Layton has to pause to frame his answer. Layton knows the comics industry thoroughly, having worked on classic runs of Marvel's Iron Man and Ant-Man in the 1980s. He also cofounded Valiant Comics.

Today, from his perch in Hollywood, Layton worries about the fate of old-fashioned comic books on paper. He notes that of the three hundred or so comics published each month, the average number of copies sold is about fifteen thousand. He emphasizes that this means most comics are not close to profitable. "I'm not an economics major but it doesn't take a Master's Degree to figure out that these numbers don't work," says Layton. "For independent publishers, this nightmare scenario keeps them hanging on by their fingernails."

The final blow, Layton believes, could come from Disney, owner of Marvel Comics. "Eventually, some middle management guy within the Disney Corporation is going to figure out that comic publishing is not very profitable," says Layton. "And, to be perfectly honest, if I was working as [a] business executive at Disney, I'd probably 'pull the plug' myself. The business side of my head can't argue with the numbers. But my heart hopes that never occurs."

Bob Layton, "What Is the Future of Comic Publishing?," Bob Layton personal website, 2023. www.boblayton.com.

for the completed book. In addition, AI is a major time saver. With its ability to perform the separate tasks of comic production all at once, it enables artists to see the finished product much more quickly. The potential for producing multiple comics in a year allows individual artists to plan and create their own series. Artist Dana Nova Darko has done just that with her AI-generated experimental eighteen-issue series *Proof of Concept*. "My brother, studying AI, introduced me to Midjourney in September 2022," says Darko. "After experimenting with the tech for a few months, I started making comic pages for fun. Initially creating faux [imitation] covers, I eventually explored full-page concepts and couldn't stop."[35]

Actually, AI's ability to speed up the creative process might be its greatest potential benefit for professional comic creators. It allows them to test out ideas like a movie director, rejecting what does not work and rapidly making changes while also keeping to a tight budget.

The DIY Approach and the Growth of Fan Comics

Artificial intelligence programs provide a major boost to the do-it-yourself, or DIY, approach to comics. This is already fueling the growth of fan comics. These are the comic book equivalent of fan fiction, in which fans write their own stories about characters from favorite TV shows and movies. One such fan comic is *Sandman: Deeper Dreams Still*, based on Neil Gaiman's hugely popular *Sandman* comics. In their introduction to the homemade comic, creators Juan Lam and Luis Larios explain what they hope to accomplish:

> This project was made with two goals in mind: to give us the opportunity to make a Sandman story of our own, and to test the limits of what AI art is capable of. *The Sandman* by Neil Gaiman is our favorite comic book, but making our own issue of *Sandman*, or any comic for that matter,

would have been too large a task for just Luis and I. . . . We hope that through this project we have made something that *is* art by using AI as one of the tools in helping us realize our vision.[36]

Using a copyrighted character without permission is illegal, but fan comics have usually not been policed in the past. Some editors have even hired writers and artists on the basis of their work on a self-produced comic. However, AI technology, with its ability to produce reams of sophisticated-looking art, threatens to make fan comics more of a competitor with genuine comics. Publishers are likely to pursue legal action against the makers of AI-generated fan comics more often now, especially if they are sold for profit.

Neil Gaiman's hugely popular Sandman *comics are the basis for a fan comic titled* Sandman: Deeper Dreams Still. *Creators of such fan comics risk being sued for copyright infringement if their products are sold for profit.*

Tech enthusiasts are also exploring new ways to use technology and crowd wisdom to make independent comics. A team of tech experts has created Forgotten Runes, a so-called decentralized franchise in which fans sign up to create their own stories based on a set group of characters. Participation in Forgotten Runes is managed by blockchain technology, in which algorithms control who shares in the franchise ownership and any profits it might make. The management team has already used the AI program ChatGPT to produce its first crowd-written comic book, *Forgotten Runes* #0. They believe that hundreds or thousands of fans and creators will be able to brainstorm plot twists and character arcs faster and more creatively than any one author. "The idea behind Forgotten Runes is that we are creating a universe, a world, and stories in the tradition of *The Lord of the Rings* and *Harry Potter*, these epic universes," says the Runes chief executive officer, who goes by the single name Dotta. "The idea here is that you can create and develop your character, but then you will actually own the commercial right to it."[37] It is hoped that the Forgotten Runes franchise will branch out into more comics, TV shows, films, games, and other genres.

WORDS IN CONTEXT

blockchain: A type of shared database that uses coded information for security

A Better Deal for Comic Artists

Amid all the technological changes in the comics industry, conditions for artists have remained mostly unchanged. Publishers still produce comics much like a factory line. Writers and artists are shuffled around like interchangeable parts, with an emphasis on rapid output.

One company, however, has introduced a new way of doing business, a template for the future of comics. Image Comics was founded in 1992 by a group of seven disgruntled artists from Marvel. The group included Todd McFarlane, Rob Liefeld, Jim Lee, Erik Larsen, Marc Silvestri, Whilce Portacio, and Jim Valentino—a who's who of the comics field, responsible for a slew of best-selling comics. They insisted that their first-class work had not earned them the profits to which they were entitled. They sought more control over working conditions and ownership of their intellectual property. Significantly, artists at other companies kept a close eye on how the Image experiment fared.

Image changed the look of comic books, with higher-quality slick paper and coloring that rivaled the best commercial art. Some of the art struck critics as being an over-the-top bid for attention, but comic fans loved it. Soon Image was producing its own hits, like *Saga*, *Savage Dragon*, *Spawn*, and *The Walking Dead*. Even more important, the company worked for its creators, rather than the other way around. Image attracted artists by promising, in exchange for a flat fee, to perform all the necessary services to take a comic from the artist's drawing board to comic stores nationwide. Image artists owned the rights to their characters themselves, with no haggling. When some of their properties were bought by Hollywood, it was the artists

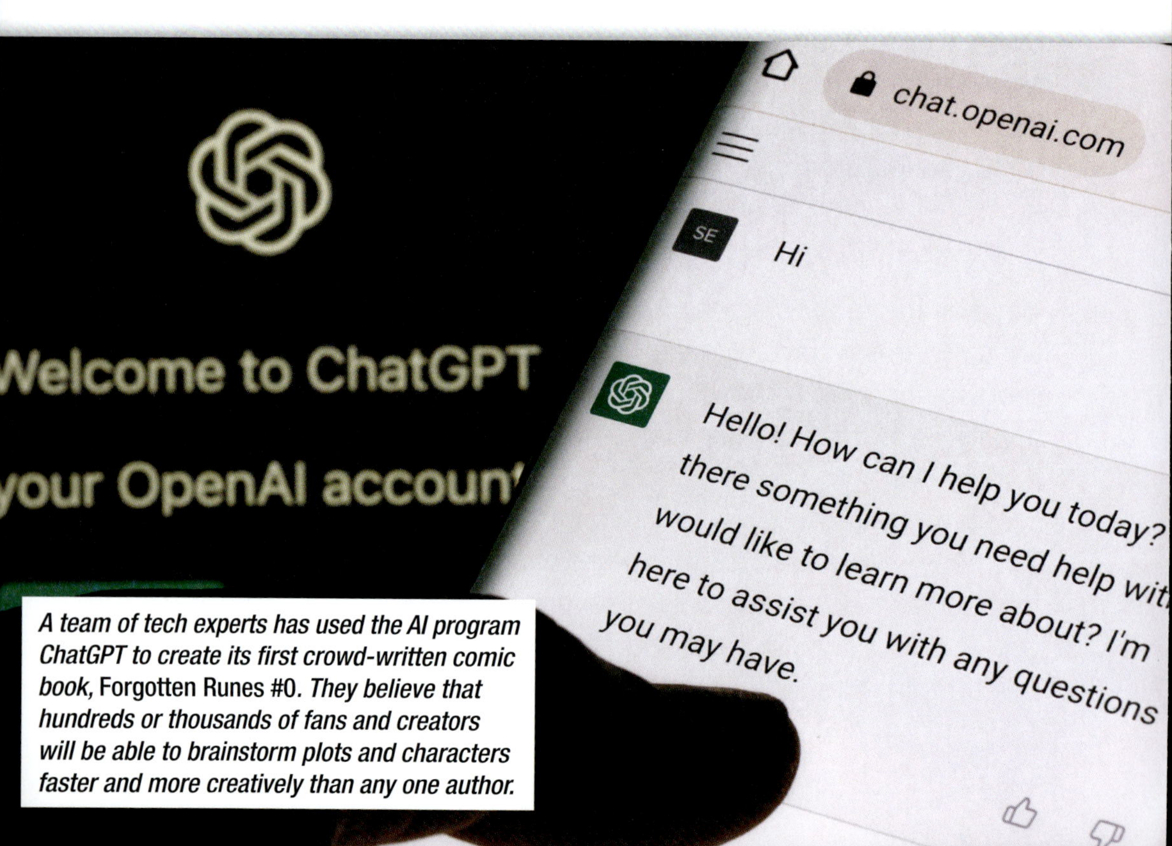

A team of tech experts has used the AI program ChatGPT to create its first crowd-written comic book, Forgotten Runes #0. *They believe that hundreds or thousands of fans and creators will be able to brainstorm plots and characters faster and more creatively than any one author.*

Helping Creators Turn Ideas into Comics

If writers have a gripping story to tell, a new California-based start-up company wants to help them turn it into a comic book. Dashtoon has devised a platform using the latest AI technology to steer storytellers' ideas into high-quality comics. Creators begin by posting a story idea to the platform and describing their main characters in detail. Next they map out the narrative on a storyboard template. From there, Dashtoon's AI program assembles the parts into a beautifully illustrated comic, ready for final editing and publication.

The Dashtoon founders—Sanidhya Narain, Lalith Gudipati, and Soumyadeep Mukherjee—believe people in the United States have unsuspected resources for storytelling, lacking only the means to illustrate their ideas. "Any storyteller, regardless of their artistic skills or technical knowledge, can create digital comics, breaking traditional barriers in illustrated content creation," says Mukherjee, who serves as the company's chief technology officer. Dashtoon's platform also streamlines the process to save time. A comic that might require forty or fifty hours of intensive work ordinarily can be completed in five or six hours. "In the coming years, the business of content will undergo many transformations," says Aakash Kumar, one of Dashtoon's investors, "and the most important of those is going to be creation getting democratized."

Quoted in David Prosser, "Meet Dashtoon, the Start-Up Helping Comic Creators to Tell Their Stories," *Forbes*, November 2, 2023. www.forbes.com.

who reaped the rewards. "Image owns no IP [intellectual property], and creators own 100% of the work they publish," says a spokesperson for the company. "They are the legal trademark and copyright owners of their work. While Image can make suggestions and provide guidance, ultimately final decisions cannot be made by Image without the creators' permission."[38]

With AI blurring the lines between amateur and professional comic artists, more pros are likely to seek working agreements like Image Comics offers. Perhaps the AI revolution and other innovations, like web comics, will lead to a new burst of creativity in the field of comic art.

Source Notes

Introduction: Telling Stories with Pictures and Words

1. Quoted in Leslie Katz, "AI Drew This Gorgeous Comics Series. You'd Never Know It," CNET, December 15, 2022. www.cnet.com.
2. Quoted in Jake Rossen, "12 Secrets of Comic Book Artists," *Mental Floss*, February 9, 2021. www.mentalfloss.com.
3. Cole Kennedy, "10 Comic Book Artists You Should Be Following in 2022," CBR, April 2, 2022. www.cbr.com.

Chapter One: A History of Comics from Newsstands to Specialty Shops

4. Quoted in Robert Downen, "Houston Man Held On to a *Superman* Comic for Years. Then He Sold It for a Record $2.6 Million," *Houston (TX) Chronicle*, December 17, 2021. www.houstonchronicle.com.
5. Quoted in Downen, "Houston Man Held On to a *Superman* Comic for Years."
6. Julia Guarneri, "How Syndicated Columns, Comics and Stories Forever Changed the News Media," *Smithsonian*, October 30, 2019. www.smithsonian.com.
7. Jill Lepore, *The Secret History of Wonder Woman*. New York: Vintage, 2015, p. xiii.
8. Quoted in Jason Stone, "Beyond Amazing: Learning from 60 Years of Spider-Man," University of Oregon. https://around.uoregon.edu.
9. Quoted in Jeremy Dauber, *American Comics: A History*. New York: Norton, 2022, p. 188.
10. Ash Chauhan, "The Fate of the Comic Book Industry: The Rise and Fall of Comic Book Stores," *Will Be Told* (blog), August 27, 2021. https://willbetold.com.

Chapter Two: Producing Comic Art

11. Quoted in *Wired*, *Todd McFarlane Answers Comics Questions from Twitter/Tech Support/*Wired, YouTube, July 18, 2023. www.youtube.com/watch?v=AUjaoK9ahA8.
12. Quoted in Nathan Cabaniss, "'I Was Making Stuff Up': *Spawn* Made Huge Lore Changes to Explain Continuity Errors," Screen Rant, May 23, 2023. https://screenrant.com.

13. *Comic Artist Resource Blog*, "The Best Pencils for Drawing Comics," July 9, 2018. https://comicartistresourceblog.com.
14. Quoted in Graphixly, "Dave Gibbons: Using Clip Studio Paint to Create Comic Book Art," May 28, 2019. https://graphixly.com.
15. Steve Ellis, "How to Layout Your Comic! Panels, Gutters, and Page Flow," Art Rocket. www.clipstudio.net.
16. CBP staff, "The Importance of Inking in Comic Art," ComicBookPros, May 22, 2023. www.comicbookpros.com.
17. David Harth, "Digital Comics vs. Print Comics: Which Is Better for You?," CBR, August 7, 2023. www.cbr.com.

Chapter Three: Skills and Career Paths for Comic Artists

18. Centers for Disease Control and Prevention, Office of Public Health Preparedness and Response, *Preparedness 101: Zombie Pandemic*, 2011. https://stacks.cdc.gov.
19. Quoted in Love Life Drawing, "Life Drawing for Comics and Cartoons—Interview with Krishna Sadasivam," 2022. www.lovelifedrawing.com.
20. Quoted in *Wired*, *Todd McFarlane Answers Comics Questions from Twitter/Tech Support/*Wired.
21. Quoted in Love Life Drawing, "Life Drawing for Comics and Cartoons—Interview with Krishna Sadasivam."
22. Quoted in Michael Dooley, "Art for Comics and Storyboards: What's the Difference?," *PRINT*, May 16, 2014. www.printmag.com.
23. Alisha Christina Moffat, "Why Webtoons Are Redefining Comics," How to Love Comics, June 29, 2022. www.howtolovecomics.com.
24. Stan Lee, *Stan Lee's Master Class*. New York: Watson-Guptill, 2019, p. 212.

Chapter Four: The Giants of Comic Art, Past and Present

25. Quoted in Robert K. Elder, "A Holy Grail in the Library of Congress: Visiting Steve Ditko's *Amazing Fantasy* #15 Original Artwork," *Comics Journal*, April 22, 2020. www.tcj.com.
26. Quoted in Elder, "A Holy Grail in the Library of Congress."
27. Randolph Hoppe, "Jack Kirby," Society of Illustrators, 2022. https://societyillustrators.org.
28. Quoted in Brian Cronin, "Will Eisner: The All-Time Greatest Title Pages from *The Spirit*," CBR, March 6, 2017. www.cbr.com.
29. Neil Gaiman, "Neil Gaiman on Will Eisner: 'He Thought Comics Were an Artform—He Was Right,'" *The Guardian* (Manchester, UK), March 7, 2017. www.theguardian.com.

30. Quoted in Alexandra Alter, "Art Spiegelman on Life with a '500-Pound Mouse Chasing Me,'" *New York Times*, December 27, 2022. www.nytimes.com.
31. Quoted in Marvel, "'Miles Morales: Spider-Man #11' Marks the Debut of Marvel Art Atelier Challenge Winner Federica Mancin," September 12, 2023. www.marvel.com.

Chapter Five: The Future of Comic Art

32. Quoted in James Hookway, "AI-Generated Comic Book 'Zarya of the Dawn' Keeps Copyright but Key Images Excluded," *Wall Street Journal*, February 24, 2023. www.wsj.com.
33. Quoted in Nathaniel Sans, "The U.S. Copyright Office's *Zarya* Decision, and the Uncertain Future of AI Comics," *Columbia Journal of Law & the Arts*, March 31, 2023. https://journals.library.columbia.edu.
34. Evan Ezquer, "The AI Revolution in Comic Books: Insights from Pioneers," Metaroids, April 9, 2023. https://metaroids.com.
35. Quoted in Ezquer, "The AI Revolution in Comic Books."
36. Juan F. Lam, "Sandman—Deeper Dreams Still," Juan Lam personal website, August 12, 2022. https://juanlam.com.
37. Quoted in Eric James Beyer, "How Forgotten Runes Is Using ChatGPT to Build a Fantasy Empire," nft now, July 7, 2023. www.nftnow.com.
38. Quoted in Gita Jackson, "The Image Union Is the Future of Comics," *Vice*, November 22, 2021. www.vice.com.

For Further Research

Books

Maury Aaseng et al., *The Art of Comic Book Drawing: More than 100 Drawing and Illustration Techniques for Rendering Comic Book Characters and Storyboards*. Laguna Beach, CA: Foster, 2020.

Jeremy Dauber, *American Comics: A History*. New York: Norton, 2022.

Nan Ji Hong and Jong Beom Lee, *Webtoon School: Everything You Need to Know About Webtoon Creation and Story Writing*. POPPYPUB, 2023.

Stan Lee, *Stan Lee's Master Class: Lessons in Drawing, World-Building, Storytelling, Manga, and Digital Comics*. New York: Watson-Guptill, 2019.

Ken Quattro, *Invisible Men: The Trailblazing Black Artists of Comic Books*. Yoe, 2020.

Internet Sources

Art Career Project, "Comic Book Artist," July 15, 2021. https://theartcareerproject.com.

J.D. Biersdorfer, "Create Your Own Digital Comics Whether You Can Draw or Not," *New York Times*, April 29, 2020. www.nytimes.com.

Benj Edwards, "AI-Generated Comic Artwork Loses US Copyright Protection," Ars Technica, February 23, 2023. https://arstechnica.com.

David Harth, "10 Ways Image Comics Changed the Industry," CBR, February 22, 2022. www.cbr.com.

David Norman, "Female Comic Book Creators," Clandestine Critic, February 14, 2021. www.clandestinecritic.co.uk.

Jake Rossen, "12 Secrets of Comic Book Artists," *Mental Floss*, February 9, 2021. www.mentalfloss.com.

Organizations and Websites

Center for Cartoon Studies (CCS)
www.teachingcomics.org
The CCS provides the highest quality of education to students interested in creating visual stories. The center emphasizes self-publishing and helps prepare its students to publish, market, and distribute their work. The CCS website contains features such as the free online comic

Cartooning in an Anxious Age, about the challenges that creative comic artists face.

Comic Book Legal Defense Fund
https://cbldf.org
The Comic Book Legal Defense Fund is a nonprofit organization dedicated to the protection of the First Amendment rights of the comic art form and its community of retailers, creators, publishers, librarians, and readers. Its website features stories about the censorship of comic artists and how they responded.

Comic-Con Museum
https://comic-conmuseum.org
The Comic-Con Museum in San Diego, California, works to increase public appreciation for comics and related popular art forms. The museum presents exhibits about comic artists past and present and provides education and maker spaces for people of all ages to learn about comic art and practice its techniques.

How to Draw Comics
www.howtodrawcomics.net
The website How to Draw Comics offers a comprehensive tutorial on the basics of creating comic art. Among its features is Clayton Barton's "Beginners Guide to Making Comics," which leads aspiring artists through the process, from "Why Draw Comics?" to "Drawing a Comic Book Page."

Jack Kirby Museum & Research Center
https://kirbymuseum.org
The Jack Kirby Museum & Research Center in New York City promotes and encourages the study, understanding, preservation, and appreciation of the work of Jack Kirby and other classic comic book artists. The museum manages a digital archive of Kirby's original artwork. It also publishes the *Kirby Effect*, a journal about Kirby and his influence on the comic book industry.

Ray & Pat Browne Library for Popular Culture Studies
www.bgsu.edu/library/pcl.html
The Ray & Pat Browne Library for Popular Culture Studies at Bowling Green State University is the most comprehensive archive of its kind in the United States. Among its materials is a wealth of information on comic books and comic art. Its website features a search tool that enables visitors to access the collection.

Index

Picture Credits

Cover: Yuravector/Shutterstock.com

7: PictureLux/The Hollywood Archive/Alamy Stock Photo
10: Courtesy of Sotheby's/MEGA/Newscom/GWGLA/Newscom
13: DC Comics/Photofest
17: Associated Press
21: Nancy Rivera/SplashNews/Newscom
24: Yura Tura/Shutterstock.com
26: Art Villone/Alamy Stock Photo
30: Golubovy/Shutterstock.com
33: Smolaw/Shutterstock.com
35: AMC/Photofest
39: Heritage Auctions/MEGA/Newscom/GWGLA/Newscom
43: Brian Cahn/ZUMA Press/Newscom
45: sjbooks/Alamy Stock Photo
49: Diego Thomazini/Shutterstock.com
52: ©Tamia Dowlatabadi
54: Ascannio/Shutterstock.com

About the Author

John Allen is a writer who lives in Oklahoma City.